America's Transition from Agriculture to Industry

Drawing Inferences and Conclusions

Greg Roza

The Rosen Publishing Group, Inc., New York

Published in 2006 by The Rosen Publishing Group, Inc.
29 East 21st Street, New York, NY 10010

First Edition

Library of Congress Cataloging-in-Publication Data

Roza, Greg.
America's transition from agriculture to industry: drawing inferences and
conclusions/Greg Roza.—1st ed.
    p. cm.—(Critical thinking in American history)
Includes index.
ISBN 1-4042-0410-5 (library binding)
1. Agriculture—Economic aspects—United States—History—Juvenile
literature. 2. Industrialization—United States—History—Juvenile literature.
3. United States—Economic conditions—Juvenile literature.
I. Title. II. Series.
HD1761.R69 2006
338.0973—dc22

2005001395

Manufactured in the United States of America

On the cover: Left: A photograph of cotton pickers on a Southern farm,
taken around 1890. Right: A 1921 image of the Edison Electric Plant in
Quincy, Massachusetts.

Contents

The First American Farmers

America's great agricultural history may never have come to be without the help and guidance of Native Americans. Native Americans enabled the European settlers to survive and prosper by teaching them effective agricultural methods. Native Americans also educated Europeans about the indigenous plants and animals of the New World. Native Americans taught the settlers to grow squash, beans, and corn. The Iroquois—who lived in the area of what is today New York State—called these crops the "three sisters" because they were often grown together in the same soil. Corn was planted first. Once the cornstalks reached a certain height, the squash and beans were planted around them. Because the squash grew close to the earth's surface, its

Q & A

Discuss the following questions with a partner.

✓ If you had been a Native American when Europeans arrived in North America, how do you think you would have felt about the newcomers? If you had been a European settler, how do you think you would have felt about the indigenous Native Americans?

✓ What do you think the Europeans thought about the Native Americans' knowledge of the land and how to plant successful crops? Can you name any other edible plants besides corn, beans, and squash that were unknown to Europeans before they settled in the New World?

✓ What do you think would have happened to the European settlers had they not received aid from Native Americans?

large leafy plants blocked the growth of weeds. As the beans grew, their vines were supported by the taller cornstalks.

Maize, or corn, was the most abundant crop planted by Native Americans. About 7,000 years ago, wild corn was more like the grasses found in the Plains states. Native Americans collected the wild corn plants best suited for eating and planted them. After Native Americans had

Colonial artist John White created this drawing of the Native American village of Secota in the company of Walter Raleigh's 1585 expedition to the New World. Researching Native Americans around the Carolina coast, White observed Native American farming, fishing, and foraging habits.

used this method for thousands of years, corn developed into the vegetable that we are familiar with today. Corn not only formed the bulk of many Native American diets, but corn husks and stalks were also widely used to make clothes, mats, and other everyday items.

Coming to America

Europeans began exploring the Western Hemisphere in the 1400s. Most were interested in finding a sea route to Asia, which was a valuable source of spices and other goods. Instead of finding a sea route, however, Christopher Columbus and other European explorers found the New World and its abundant resources. By the early 1600s, several European countries had established colonies in the New World with dreams of fortune, power, and adventure.

In 1607, about 100 British settlers founded Jamestown, the first permanent British settlement in the state known today as Virginia. Other Europeans soon established colonies, too. These original settlers faced great hardships. Many died from disease and starvation. They soon discovered, however, that their new home was suitable for farming. The soil was fertile, sources of

Fact Finders

Search for the answers to these questions as you read the text.

✓ What was the first permanent British settlement in the United States, and when was it founded?

✓ In what ways was the land of the New World ideal for farming?

✓ In what ways did Native Americans aid British settlers?

This is a re-creation of the Jamestown colony in Virginia. Although Jamestown was the first permanent British settlement in the New World, diseases such as typhoid fever and cholera ravaged its inhabitants since colonists were depositing waste into and also drinking from the nearby James River.

water and minerals were plentiful, and the moderate weather was ideal for steady growth. Although many of the plants the settlers brought with them from Europe adapted poorly to the new environment, the settlers soon began to cultivate the local flora using Native American farming methods. In the years that followed, new technologies and tools helped the British colonies develop into a great source of wealth for Great Britain.

The Growth of Colonial Farms

Throughout the 1600s, Europeans flocking to the Western Hemisphere found a seemingly limitless expanse of fertile land on which to start farms. By the 1630s, many Dutch farmers had settled in New Netherland, the area that is today New York, New Jersey, Delaware, and Connecticut. The Dutch West India Company granted a large estate to anyone who brought at least fifty adults to New Netherland during a four-year period. The landowner—or patroon—provided his tenants with livestock, tools, and buildings. In return, tenants worked the land, paid rent, and gave surplus crops to the patroon. The patroon system failed because few people wanted to give up their freedom. Soon the Dutch West India Company offered free land in New Netherland to anyone who paid his or her own passage to America.

As early as 1619, slaves from Africa were brought to the colony of Virginia to work on plantations—vast

Paper Work

The United States is a country founded on the concept of freedom; the U.S. Constitution states "all men are created equal." Yet by 1860, approximately one-third of the people in the Southern states were African slaves. Slavery was an important factor in American farming and economics. Consider these questions as you write an essay about the relationship between the emergence of the United States as an agricultural country and its approval of slavery.

✓ How has slavery shaped early agriculture in the United States?

✓ How do you think U.S. agriculture would be different today if slavery had never been allowed in the colonies?

Uncle Tom.

farms that usually grew a single crop. Plantations gained a strong foothold in the agricultural and financial landscape of the colonies, and the use

These two items show that slavery was once common in America. At left is an engraving of slaves processing tobacco leaves at a Virginia farm. At right is an advertisement in the form of a cigarette card showing the literary character Uncle Tom. *Uncle Tom's Cabin*, a novel by Harriet Beecher Stowe, drew attention to the antislavery cause during the 1850s.

of slave labor became a widespread practice. Although the plantation system resulted in the rapid settlement and population of the Southern colonies, most plantation slaves were condemned to a life of forced labor.

Colonial Cash Crops

As farms became more widespread in North America, fur trading—once a common moneymaking venture—was replaced by the sale of cash crops. The crops grown in the colonies that brought in a profit include tobacco, corn, wheat, rice, cotton, and indigo.

Tobacco—grown initially in Virginia and Maryland—was the colonies' largest cash crop. This was both a benefit and a curse in the historical development of the colonies that would eventually become the United States. Grown in Virginia as early as 1612, tobacco quickly became a highly prof-itable export. Tobacco became so valuable in the colonies and overseas that it was often used as a form of cur-rency well into the eighteenth century. However, it was this demand for tobacco that made slavery a popular means of cultivating

These farmworkers are harvesting tobacco leaves on a Virginia plantation. Slaves had no rights and were dependent on their masters for everything, including shoes, clothes, and food.

Get Graphic

Use the chart to answer the questions below:

✓ What centuries does this chart cover?

✓ Between which two years on this chart was there the greatest jump in tobacco imported to England from America? What was the cause of this increase?

✓ What does this data tell you about the importance of slavery to the tobacco trade in the colonial economy?

English Tobacco Imported from America

Year	Millions of Pounds
1620	0.1
1630	0.5
1672	17.6
1682	21.4
1688	28.4
1708	30
1717	32
1722	35
1730	41
1740	41
1745	55
1755	64
1760	85
1775	102

the plant quickly and inexpensively. Many tobacco plantations grew at the cost of African slaves who were forced to leave their country and family and work under brutal conditions.

The Agricultural Revolution

A revolution in agriculture began in England in the mid-1700s. An important transition in farming occurred from hand labor to machine labor, and from subsistence farming to commercial farming. The three most influential discoveries were improved growing practices (especially crop rotation), new livestock-breeding methods, and the invention of new farm equipment.

While most of the agricultural innovations were developed in England, American colonists developed some important farm tools. In 1794, for instance, Eli Whitney invented the cotton gin, which was a

Word Works

✓ **commercial farming** A system of farming on a large scale that produces an abundance of goods for sale and export to other places.

✓ **innovation** A new idea, method, or tool.

✓ **revolution** A sudden, radical, or complete change.

✓ **subsistence farming** A system of farming that provides most of the goods a family needs to live with little or no surplus for sale.

✓ **transform** To change the form or appearance of something. (The word "transform" is a verb. "Transformation" is a noun that means "the act or process of transforming.")

Eli Whitney's cotton gin changed the scale of American farming from small plantations to large enterprises. Because the plantations were cultivating a single crop—cotton—the cotton gin produced as much as 50 pounds (23 kilograms) of cotton per day.

machine that separated cotton fiber from cotton seeds. This invention made the large-scale production of cotton possible, and allowed cotton to surpass tobacco as the leading cash crop of the Southern colonies. In 1834, Cyrus McCormick patented the first successful reaping machine, which made grain harvesting easier. These are just two of many agricultural innovations created by American inventors.

These inventions enabled the American colonies to thrive as agricultural producers. Farming became more profitable, and more farms sprang up throughout the colonies. The colonies of North America were beginning to develop from individual settlements into a network of agricultural centers. This transformation marked the beginning of the American Industrial Revolution, which would eventually help the United States become the powerful nation that it is today.

Samuel Slater

Samuel Slater was born in England on June 6, 1768. He became an apprentice at a textile mill at the age of fourteen. During the next seven years, Slater learned everything about the textile business. In 1789, Slater took his knowledge of the English textile industry and secretly moved to Pawtucket, Rhode Island. While other Englishmen with knowledge of the textile business had moved to the colonies before him, Slater was the first who knew how to build and use textile machines. In 1793, with the aid of local builders and investors, Slater built the first water-driven textile mill in the colonies.

As Slater's textile mill grew, he developed a system of business that encouraged growth. He hired workers—mostly children—to work in his factory. As his workforce expanded, he established a community

Fact Finders

Search the text for the answers to these questions as you read the text.

✓ What set Slater apart from other Englishmen who had traveled to America to start textile businesses? Why had he succeeded when others had struggled?

✓ Why has Slater been called the father of America's Industrial Revolution? Based on the facts presented in the text, would you agree or disagree with that title? Explain.

This is a depiction of Samuel Slater's cotton mill. Armed with a large inheritance and the experience of having worked for years in a textile mill in England, Slater knew he would be a success if he took his knowledge of the industry to America.

for his workers and their families. He built houses, company stores, schools, and churches. This community attracted new workers, and Slater's business flourished. This method of business, which became known as the Rhode Island system, became popular throughout New England. Samuel Slater has been called the father of America's Industrial Revolution because his mechanical innovations and unique methods started America on the path to industrial greatness.

Taming the Frontier

Once the United States won the American Revolution, colonists eagerly turned their attention to the unsettled frontier. With the aid of American military forces, many farmers immediately took control of fertile lands that had long been home to Native Americans. In the early 1800s, farms and settlements sprang up around the Great Lakes and along the Mississippi and Ohio rivers. These waterways became vital transportation routes for shipping goods to cities and ports back east and overseas.

On July 13, 1787, Congress passed the Northwest Ordinance. This law declared that the area north of the Ohio River and east of the Mississippi River (called the Northwest Territory) would be admitted to the Union when it met certain conditions regarding population

Word Works

✓ **fertile** Rich in material needed to support plant growth.

✓ **frontier** A region beyond settled territory.

✓ **ordinance** A law.

✓ **petition** To make a formal request.

✓ **squatter** A person who settles on property without the permission of its owner.

✓ **territory** A section of land under the protection and control of a government.

and government. This area was an ideal place to grow crops such as wheat and corn. Settlers purchased the cheap, fertile land from the government and flocked to the area to set up family farms. Squatters who could not afford land set up homes and farms without permission, and then petitioned the government for ownership of the land. The area eventually became the states of Ohio, Indiana, Illinois, Michigan, and Wisconsin. The Northwest Ordinance became a blueprint for the settlement of later territories, and America's available farmland stretched farther west.

THOMAS JEFFERSON'S *Conception*

FOR THE SUBDIVISION OF THE NEW WEST. THIS PROPOSAL WAS CONTEMPORARY WITH HIS ORDINANCE OF 1784 FOR THE GOVERNMENT OF NORTHWEST TERRITORY, BUT WHICH NEVER BECAME EFFECTIVE

Except for the classical names for states, note how prophetic the plan Jefferson had never seen the West.

This unusual plan for proposed states in America was put forth by Thomas Jefferson in 1784. Jefferson wanted to divide the nation in a grid that yielded fourteen states with names like Metropotamia, Pelisipia, and Illinoia. Instead, Congress passed the Northwest Ordinance of 1787.

The Erie Canal and Buffalo, New York

Frontier settlers in the West needed a constant flow of new supplies from the East. Consumers and merchants on the East Coast wanted the goods of the western settlements. However, the roads were poor, and the existing water routes were inconvenient. Americans sought more efficient modes of transportation.

Completed in 1825, the Erie Canal made transportation quicker, cheaper, and easier. Because of the canal, towns in New York that had once been small and inaccessible—such as Syracuse, Rochester, and Buffalo—flourished into modern industrial centers. The canal also attracted more settlers to the western frontier, including the steadily increasing flow of immigrants arriving in the United States.

Buffalo became a major gateway between the vast agricultural areas of the West and the industrial cities of the East. People traveling west reached the

Get Graphic

Use this map of New York State and the Erie Canal to answer the following questions.

✓ Identify Buffalo and Albany on the map and then use your finger to trace the solid line between these cities. This is the Erie Canal.

✓ Note the location of the states surrounding the canal. How do you think farming in these states was influenced by the canal?

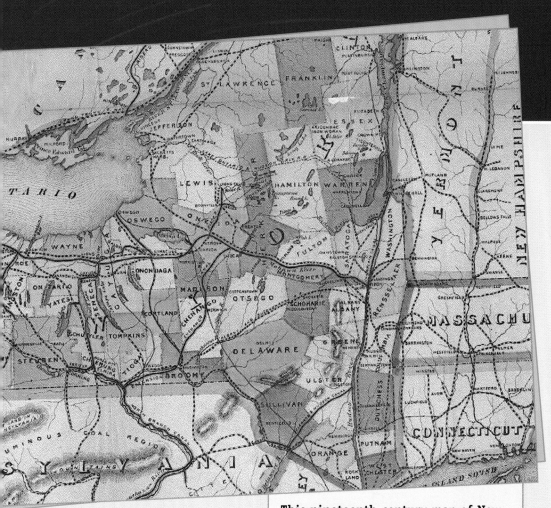

This nineteenth-century map of New York State outlines its canals and railroads in 1866. New York was transformed after the installation of the Erie Canal, which linked the city of Buffalo with the Great Lakes region.

end of the canal in Buffalo and then continued their journey in wagons. Farmers flocked to Buffalo with wagons filled with produce and raw materials destined for eastern ports. In 1842, Buffalo boasted the first steam-driven grain elevator in the world. By 1863, Buffalo had a total of twenty-seven grain elevators. The Erie Canal and grain elevators helped to make Buffalo a major producer of flour and the largest grain port in the world.

Factories Versus Plantations

American politicians struggled to strengthen the economy in the years just after the American Revolution. Skillful leadership and bountiful natural resources helped provide the country with a solid economy. Southern plantation owners became rich from selling their crops in the United States and overseas. The enormous cotton and tobacco plantations required a large number of slave laborers. Because plantation owners did not pay their workers, they grew even wealthier.

Although farming remained the main occupation in the North, Northern farms were smaller than Southern plantations and did not require as many

Fact Finders

Look for the answers to these questions as you read the text.

✓ What was the main occupation in the South after the American Revolution?

✓ What was the main occupation in the North after the American Revolution?

✓ Why didn't Northern farms need large teams of laborers like Southern farms needed?

✓ What were two reasons for the start of the American Civil War?

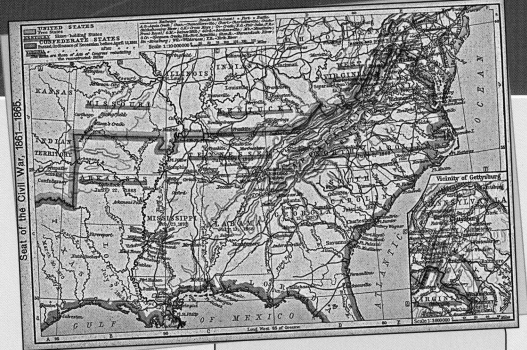

By the time of the Missouri Compromise in 1820, the Southern and Northern states were divided on the issue of slavery. Although the compromise was put forth to help avoid the question of slavery, it remained unsolved.

laborers. Other industries, such as manufacturing and banking, began to take center stage in the North. Factories began to fill Northern cities where the economy was slowly transforming from one based on agriculture to one based on industry.

The abolitionist movement against slavery, which had originated in colonial times, gained momentum in the North. Most Southerners fiercely defended slavery, which had become the foundation of their economic system. Without it, they argued, the economy of the South would crumble. The arguments over slavery and the differing economies of the North and the South were two of the reasons for the start of the American Civil War (1861–1865).

Agriculture and Industry During the Civil War

Both agriculture and industry played important roles during the American Civil War. By 1861, the North had more than two times the population of the South. This was because of the steady stream of European immigrants who moved to the United States in the nineteenth century. Because of this abundant workforce, the North maintained a flourishing industrial economy. New inventions, such as the sewing machine, and new manufacturing methods, such as mass production, also helped the North produce more supplies and better weapons for their troops than the South. The North transported supplies on new railroad lines and sent messages to the front over new telegraph lines. Northern farms and factories increased production to meet wartime needs. Because of these industrial developments, the North was better prepared for a long-term war.

The South had the wealth to fund a war, but it lacked the superior

Get Graphic

Use the graphs and pie chart to answer the questions below.

✓ How many people lived in the North in 1861? How many lived in the South?

✓ How many factories were in the North in 1861? In the South?

✓ How many more miles of railroad track were in the North than in the South in 1861?

✓ What do these graphs tell you about the North and the South at the start of the American Civil War?

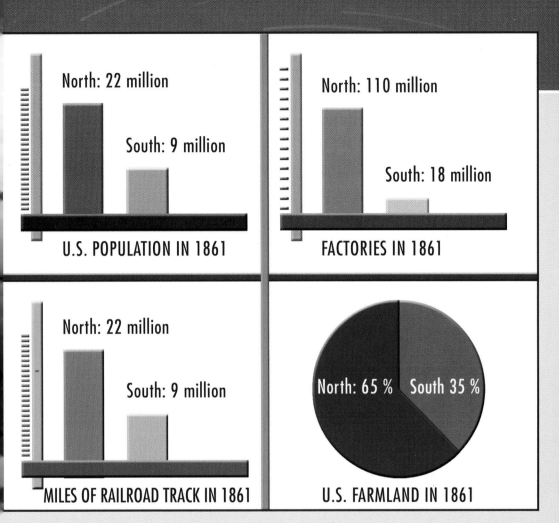

North: 22 million

South: 9 million

U.S. POPULATION IN 1861

North: 110 million

South: 18 million

FACTORIES IN 1861

North: 22 million

South: 9 million

MILES OF RAILROAD TRACK IN 1861

North: 65 %   South 35 %

U.S. FARMLAND IN 1861

manpower or technology of the North. Cotton production in the South was reduced in order to focus energies on food production to feed troops. The Civil War was fought primarily in the middle and Southern states. Many Southern plantations were destroyed during Civil War battles, leaving Southern troops hungry and poorly supplied. By the end of the war, the South's railroads were nearly at a standstill. These circumstances helped the North win the war in 1865.

How the Civil War Changed America

The South was in ruins at the end of the Civil War. Many Southern towns, once admired for their beauty and architecture, had been leveled. Their means of industry and trade were demolished. Many Americans, Northerners and Southerners, blacks and whites, flocked to cities to find employment. The cities grew larger and manufacturing boomed as the nation quickly got back on its feet. Others moved west to establish new farmsteads and to help settle the frontier. Historians believe the results of the Civil War catapulted the United States into a position of power among world economies.

With the end of slavery, Southern plantations needed new systems of labor. Many Southern farmers turned to sharecropping. A sharecropper worked the land on a large farm. In return, he or she received a share of the money made from the sale of the crops. However, plantation owners were able to keep their workers in

Q & A

Write down your answers to these questions from the specific viewpoints of a sharecropper, a slave, and someone moving to a city. Form a small group of students. Take turns reading your answers. Discuss your various opinions within the group.

✓ Why do you think so many people moved into cities at the end of the Civil War?

✓ Compare and contrast slavery and sharecropping. Is one system of labor better than the other? Explain.

During and just after the Civil War, many Southerners flocked to Northern cities like New York, which is seen in this 1862 photograph. After the Southern economies were largely disrupted, Southerners headed north in search of lucrative jobs.

debt by allowing them to open accounts at the plantation's general store, and then continuously charge high prices for goods. Similar to slavery, sharecropping allowed plantation owners to dominate their workers while paying them little or nothing for their work. Initially, most sharecroppers were former slaves, but soon many poor white people became sharecroppers, too.

CHAPTER 4: **The Industrial Revolution**

Think Tank

The previous chapters of this book have already mentioned several developments of the Industrial Revolution:

- cotton gins
- Erie Canal
- factories
- grain elevators
- mass production
- railroads
- Rhode Island system
- steam-driven machinery

✓ Form a small group of classmates. Select a topic from the list above. Use this book, other books, and the Internet to research that topic.

✓ Assign one of these roles to each of the students in your group: researcher, writer, artist, and presenter.

✓ Prepare a five-minute presentation. Include a description of the topic, an explanation of how it was used, a graphic (drawing, graph, etc.), and your thoughts on its importance to the American Industrial Revolution.

What Was the Industrial Revolution?

The Industrial Revolution began in England in the 1700s and spread throughout Europe and North America in the early 1800s. It was an era of technological advancements that led to an increase in production in many areas of life. The Industrial Revolution was a turning point in the history of mankind. It marked the transformation of the Western world from a rural, agricultural society to an urban, industrial society.

American industries after the Civil War grew rapidly due

to technological innovations and improved methods of transportation and communication. Inventors created machines that increased production. New railroads could transport goods from one coast to the other more quickly and easily than ever before. Bankers and wealthy businessmen invested large

In this photograph taken in 1863, the U.S. Military Railroad Construction Corps is repairing the Orange and Alexandria Railroad in Virginia. This particular line served as a supply train for both Confederate and Union troops during the Civil War.

amounts of money in new businesses, allowing them to grow and prosper. Several cornerstones of modern American commerce were established in the first years of the Industrial Revolution, including the coal, petroleum, steel, automobile, and clothing industries.

American agriculture benefited from the industrial advancements as well. New tools and machines made farming easier, more productive, and less expensive. Thanks to new modes of transportation and communication, farmers were better able to settle the western frontier and build stable lives for themselves while improving the U.S. economy.

Agriculture During the Industrial Revolution

The Industrial Revolution partly arose out of a need for improved agricultural methods. Innovations made farming in America more profitable and productive. New and improved farm tools, such as the seed drill, the combine, and the automatic wire binder, made managing crops quicker and easier. Improved farming methods, including crop rotation and selective animal breeding, made farming even more fruitful. Improved transportation allowed farmers to move their produce to markets more quickly and more often. By the early 1900s, American farmers benefited from gasoline-powered vehicles, pesticides, and fertilizer.

While the changes caused by the Industrial Revolution were beneficial to the U.S. economy and its

Word Works

✓ **combine** A farm machine that separates the seed from grain as it harvests the grain.

✓ **eclipse** To surpass or do better than.

✓ **fertilizer** A material added to soil to make it more nutrient rich.

✓ **migrate** To move from one region to another, often as part of a large group.

✓ **pesticide** A substance used to kill pests, such as those that eat crops.

Advancements in equipment made farms of every size more profitable. As farm owners became more reliant on machines, however, there were far fewer jobs for human laborers. This image shows farmers in Minnesota during the early 1900s.

expansion, they caused the importance of agriculture to the U.S. economy to decline. The area of land used for farming in America expanded greatly, as did the number of people working on farms. However, the growth of manufacturing swiftly eclipsed agriculture. New inventions and methods like those already mentioned meant that farms needed fewer workers. Many rural people migrated to cities to find work in the multitude of factories that seemed to spring up overnight. Between 1790 and the end of the nineteenth century, the number of people working on American farms dropped from 75 to 40 percent of the national workforce.

Industrial Developments in America

[Hundreds of inventions were produced during the American Industrial Revolution. A handful of truly groundbreaking innovations drastically changed everyday life in America and around the world.] In 1844, Samuel Morse invented the first electric telegraph, making communication over long distances as easy as dots and dashes. On May 10, 1869, the Union Pacific and Central Pacific railroad companies finished constructing the first transcontinental railroad in Promontory, Utah, making transportation easier and quicker. In 1876, Alexander Graham Bell patented his revolutionary telephone. By 1884, long-distance telephone connections were established between Boston, Massachusetts, and New York, New York. Thomas Edison invented several important inventions during his life, perhaps the

Paper Work

Select one of the innovations mentioned in the text. Research the invention at the library or on the Internet. Write an essay explaining how the invention has changed or shaped progress in the United States. Use the following questions as a guide:

✓ Why was there a need for this invention?

✓ Was this invention an instant success, or did it take time for it to catch on?

✓ How has this invention helped to shape U.S. society?

✓ How would your life today be different if this invention had never been created?

Although the transition from steam-powered to gasoline-powered tractors was slow, superior growth in crop production was noted after the switch. In this photograph, farmers pose with their new tractors, manufactured using Henry Ford's assembly-line method.

most influential of which was the lightbulb in 1879.

In 1896, George Westinghouse created the first hydroelectric generators at Niagara Falls. The electricity created by these generators was used to power the first streetlights in the world in Buffalo, New York, more than 20 miles (32.2 kilometers) away. In 1903, Henry Ford founded the Ford Motor Company. Within a decade, Ford built the first moving assembly line and implemented the use of interchangeable parts to build his automobiles. Ford's practices helped usher the United States into a new era of industrial productivity.

Problems of the Industrial Revolution

The Industrial Revolution resulted in a distancing of the social classes in America. Kings of industry, such as oil magnate John D. Rockefeller and railroad tycoon Andrew Carnegie, lived in lavish homes resembling European castles. Their large corporations devoured small businesses, forming a handful of powerful monopolies. Those who supported these businessmen, many of whom were corrupt politicians, called them captains of industry; their critics called them robber barons.

While wealthy businessmen grew richer, poor Americans and immigrants lived in filthy and crowded city neighborhoods. Cities became so

Think Tank

Prepare for a class role-playing experiment by researching the Haymarket Riot of 1886. Divide the students into various roles: one factory owner, one factory manager, four police officers, and two union leaders. The remaining students will be factory workers. The scene is a factory workers' strike. The factory workers want to establish an eight-hour workday. Consider these questions as you role-play within the group:

✓ What do the union leaders say to the factory workers? What do the union leaders say to the factory manager and/or factory owner? How do they react to the union leaders' words?

✓ What do the manager and/or factory owner say to the factory workers? How do they react?

✓ What role do the police play in the strike?

✓ Is the outcome beneficial or harmful to the plight of the factory workers?

This colored engraving depicts Chicago's famous Haymarket Riot, a dispute between union leaders and workers that resulted in a bomb explosion in May 1886. Although it was never determined who was responsible for the violence, seven police officers died and sixty-seven other police officers and workers were injured.

overcrowded that there were not enough homes or jobs for everyone. Water and air pollution caused by factories became a problem, as did dangerous working conditions within the factories. Wages were pitiful. Children as young as ten years of age often worked twelve-hour days, six days a week, instead of attending school.

Beginning in the mid-1800s, labor unions attempted to help working people achieve better wages, shorter working hours, and safer workplace conditions. Union strikes often resulted in violence and destruction. Unions struggled for nearly sixty years to improve working conditions and did not meet with widespread success until the early 1900s.

Westward Expansion

Throughout the 1800s, the policy of Manifest Destiny, the belief that Americans had a divine right to expand the country farther west, became more popular. Many Americans believed that the United States had a God-given right to rule all of North America due to its political and economic superiority. The United States purchased vast tracts of land from European countries, such as the Louisiana Territory in 1803. It also took land through warfare, such as the land it received from Mexico at the end of the Mexican-American War in 1848.

Many Americans and immigrants rushed to California in

Paper Work

Manifest Destiny was the belief that America had the right to dominate the Northern Hemisphere. The phrase was coined in 1845 by an editor named John L. O'Sullivan. O'Sullivan wrote in an article: "[T]he right of our manifest destiny to over spread and to possess the whole of the continent which Providence has given us for the development of the great experiment of liberty and federative development of self government entrusted to us."

1. With the help of a dictionary, rewrite O'Sullivan's quote in your own words.
2. After translating the quote, write a paragraph that answers the following questions:
   a. How did the philosophy of Manifest Destiny guide the agricultural and industrial development of the United States?
   b. How do you think the United States would be different today if it had not followed a philosophy of Manifest Destiny?

This map of the United States and its possessions shows territorial growth from the original thirteen colonies. America expanded west as a result of negotiated settlements, forced annexations, and financial agreements. The Native American populations who once thrived on the same lands diminished greatly.

the late 1840s and early 1850s during the California gold rush. While few people actually struck it rich, many settled in California and farmed the land. Widespread farming on the prairies west of the Mississippi River began in the 1850s. Government policies like the Homestead Act of 1862 granted families free or inexpensive land on the Plains provided that they lived on and worked the land for a number of years. Innovations like barbed wire helped farmers establish productive cattle ranches and farms. By the 1890s, the frontier was settled, and cities emerged from the wilderness.

Government Aid in the Early 1900s

In the 1900s, many forests in the Great Plains had been burned to make room for crops, and much of the land had been overgrazed. A large stretch of farmland on the Great Plains, the Dust Bowl, suffered from soil erosion due to the overproduction of crops. The region also experienced droughts and dust storms that destroyed crops. In the 1930s, the federal government set up the Soil Conservation Service to educate farmers about soil erosion. It established flood prevention and irrigation systems, and planted more than 18,500 miles (29,773 km) of trees to help prevent windstorms. Some farmers were paid to let their farmland idle, or sit unused for a period. This allowed overworked soil to become fertile again.

The period was also a difficult time

Think Tank

Split the class into two groups of students.

✓ Group one: You are farmers from Kansas in 1936.

✓ Group two: You are a group of factory workers from Chicago, Illinois, in 1936.

✓ Use the library and the Internet to research Dust Bowl farmers/Great Depression factory workers during the 1930s.

✓ Group one: Prepare a short presentation explaining your life before and after the Soil Conservation Service. Explain how it has helped to improve your quality of life.

✓ Group two: Prepare a short presentation explaining your life before and after the National Labor Relations Act of 1935. Explain how it has helped to improve your quality of life.

for industrial workers. Wages were low, and many people used credit to buy things they needed, leading them into debt. This eventually resulted in a sharp decrease in American spending.

In this Depression-era photograph, thousands of unemployed men line up at the emergency unemployment relief office in New York City. One of the results of the Industrial Revolution was a period of economic instability.

The Great Depression of the 1930s left many Americans jobless and penniless. In 1932, Franklin D. Roosevelt became president. With his plainly spoken message, "The only thing we have to fear is fear itself," he helped the American people regain their spirit in the midst of the economic crisis with his New Deal. Among our nation's greatest reformers, Roosevelt granted emergency loans to failing banks and businesses, employed people in capital projects, and assisted farmers. Roosevelt also began unemployment compensation programs, social security, a basic minimum wage, and low-rent housing opportunities. The National Labor Relations Act of 1935 also gave factory workers the right to form unions and to engage in collective bargaining. This resulted in better working conditions, fairer wages, and a stronger U.S. economy.

The Transformation of America

The Founding Fathers of the United States believed in the principles of patriotism, hard work, ingenuity, and high achievement. These ideals were woven into the fabric of the United States as it grew. After the American Revolution, the annual population of the United States increased dramatically due to a steady pouring of immigrants to its shores. In fact, the height of immigration from Europe to the United States between 1880 and 1910 is one of the most important factors that determined its success as a world leader. While the expansive frontier contained fertile farmland, plants, animals, freshwater, ores, metals, and minerals, it was the wealth of human power that swiftly tamed the wilderness, capitalizing on its natural resources.

Thanks in part to the ideals on which the country was founded, a continually growing workforce, and an abundance of natural resources, the United States was soon able to lead the world in industrial innovations, manufacturing, and commerce. Because of

Q & A

Team up with a classmate and take turns asking and answering the following questions.

✓ Which of the following do you think is most responsible for shaping the United States into the nation that it is today: leadership, steadily increasing population, land and resources, industrial capabilities, or national pride? Explain your answer.

✓ Which do you think is most important to the U.S. economy today: agriculture or industry? Explain your answer.

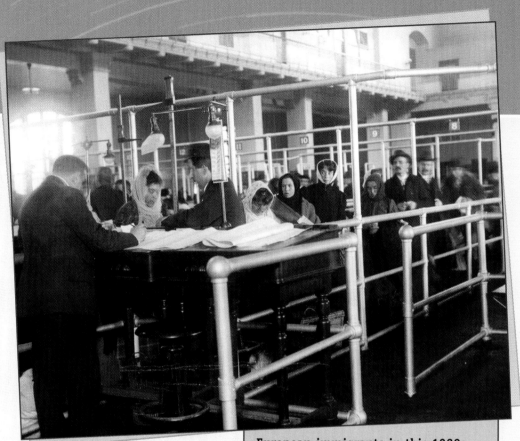

European immigrants in this 1920s photograph are being processed at Ellis Island. Large-scale immigration to America throughout the nineteenth and twentieth centuries was among the greatest reasons for our nation's later success as a world leader in manufacturing.

industrial developments, American agriculture became highly efficient and productive, even though the number of farms and farmers declined. Large corporations known as agribusinesses soon dominated modern American agriculture, and small family farms became less common.

Today, the United States is a world leader in both industry and agriculture, but industry has taken center stage in the U.S. economy. In just 200 years, America transformed from a small group of rural, agricultural colonies into a vast, industrial powerhouse.

Timeline

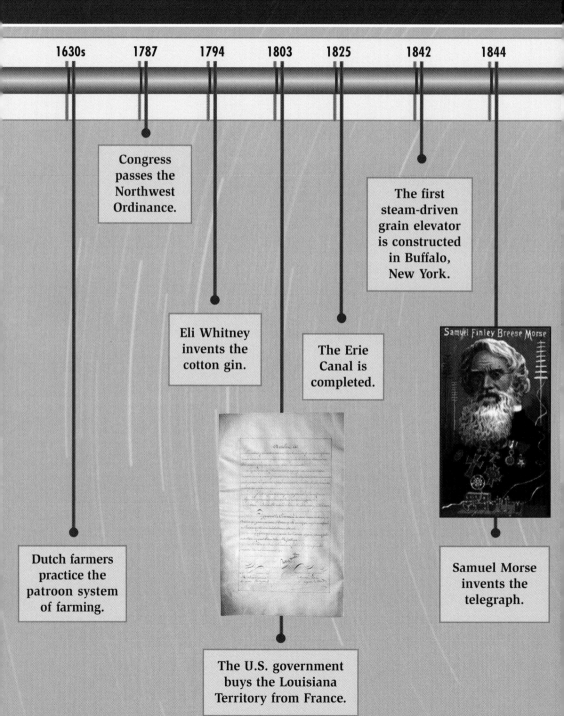

1630s   **1787**   **1794**   **1803**   **1825**   **1842**   **1844**

Congress passes the Northwest Ordinance.

The first steam-driven grain elevator is constructed in Buffalo, New York.

Eli Whitney invents the cotton gin.

The Erie Canal is completed.

Samuel Finley Breese Morse

Dutch farmers practice the patroon system of farming.

Samuel Morse invents the telegraph.

The U.S. government buys the Louisiana Territory from France.

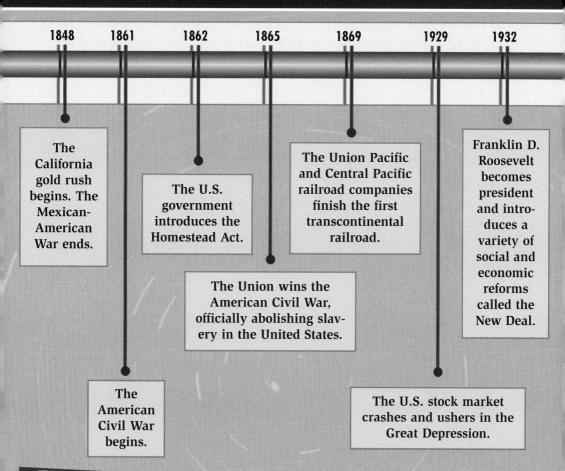

| 1848 | 1861 | 1862 | 1865 | 1869 | 1929 | 1932 |

The California gold rush begins. The Mexican-American War ends.

The U.S. government introduces the Homestead Act.

The Union Pacific and Central Pacific railroad companies finish the first transcontinental railroad.

Franklin D. Roosevelt becomes president and introduces a variety of social and economic reforms called the New Deal.

The Union wins the American Civil War, officially abolishing slavery in the United States.

The American Civil War begins.

The U.S. stock market crashes and ushers in the Great Depression.

Get Graphic

Use the timeline to answer the following questions.

✓ What single U.S. capital transportation project listed here greatly influenced the Industrial Revolution? How many years passed between the completion of the Erie Canal and the completion of the first transcontinental railroad?

✓ What event began the country's greatest economic depression? What was Franklin D. Roosevelt's plan to counteract its devastating effects?

Graphic Organizers in Action

Venn Diagram: Slavery Versus Sharecropping

SLAVERY

✓ African slaves were forced to do all work on plantations

✓ Slaves did not receive pay, land, or a share of the crops

✓ Southern states became very wealthy under this system

✓ Both systems allowed plantation owners to keep laborers in a type of servitude

✓ Cotton and tobacco were the main crops under both systems

SHARECROPPING

✓ Used "free" labor

✓ Laborers received a share of the profits

✓ Southern economy struggled under this system

CAUSE
Cotton production was reduced in the South to help grow food for troops.

CAUSE
By 1861, the North had twice the population of the South.

CAUSE
The North had a blossoming industrial economy. It was able to produce more supplies and better weapons for its troops.

CAUSE
Most battles were fought in the Southern states, resulting in the destruction of many Southern towns and plantations.

EFFECT
The North won the American Civil War.

CAUSE
The North had new railroads and new telegraph lines, making travel and communication faster and easier.

CAUSE
By the end of the war, Southern railroads were nearly at a standstill.

CAUSE
Northern farms and factories increased production to meet wartime needs.

Series of Events Chain: Buffalo, New York:
The Largest Grain-Handling Port in the World

Americans settled the frontier after the American Revolution. The frontier had plentiful natural resources.

U.S. Congress passed the Northwest Ordinance, which declared that the land between the Ohio and Mississippi rivers would eventually be admitted into the Union. This law became a model for admitting frontier territories into the Union, helping the United States expand.

Frontier towns grew quickly, but transportation was difficult. Roads were in poor condition. Water routes were inconvenient.

The Erie Canal was completed in 1825. The canal, which ended in Buffalo, New York, made transportation to and from the frontier much quicker, cheaper, and easier.

Frontier farmers began flocking to Buffalo with wagons of grain to be shipped to eastern cities and ports.

The first steam-driven grain elevator was constructed in Buffalo, New York, in 1842. By 1863, Buffalo was the largest grain-handling port in the world.

Get Graphic

✓ The series of events chain shows the events that resulted in Buffalo, New York, becoming the largest grain-handling port in the world in 1863. Can you create a series of events chain to illustrate the events that led up to the establishment of the Soil Conservation Service?

Glossary

abolition (ah-boh-LIH-shun) The elimination of the system of slavery.

collective bargaining (kuh-LEK-tiv BAR-gan-ing) Negotiation between an employer and a union leader.

conservation (kahn-sur-VAY-shun) The careful protection and preservation of natural resources.

fertile (FUR-tiyl) Capable of sustaining abundant plant growth.

hydroelectric (hy-dro-ee-LEK-trik) Relating to electricity created by waterpower.

indentured servant (in-DEN-churd SER-vunt) One who works for another for a specified period of time to repay a debt.

indigenous (in-DIJ-en-us) Occurring naturally in a particular region or environment.

indigo (IN-di-go) A plant from which blue dye is made.

ingenuity (in-jen-OO-ih-tee) Skill and cleverness in conceiving of a plan.

labor union (LAY-bor YOON-yun) An organization of workers formed for the purpose of protecting its members from unfair working conditions.

monopoly (muh-NAH-poh-lee) A company or individual that has exclusive control over the distribution of a good or service.

New Deal (NOO DEEL) The social and economic policies initiated by President Franklin D. Roosevelt in the 1930s to help save the United

States from the Great Depression by creating jobs, better living conditions, improved wages, and a stronger economy.

subsistence (sub-SIS-tens) Referring to the minimum food and shelter needed to sustain life.

technology (tek-NAH-loh-jee) The practical application of knowledge, and the specialized field to which that knowledge applies.

textile (TEX-tiyl) A woven or knit cloth.

Web Sites

Due to the changing nature of Internet links, the Rosen Publishing Group, Inc., has developed an online list of Web sites related to the subject of this book. This site is updated regularly. Please use this link to access the list.

http://www.rosenlinks.com/ctah/atai

For Further Reading

Collins, Mary. *The Industrial Revolution*. Danbury, CT: Scholastic Publishing, 2000.

Colman, Penny. *Strike!: The Bitter Struggle of American Workers from Colonial Times to the Present*. Brookfield, CT: Millbrook Press, 1995.

Levy, Janey. *The Erie Canal: A Primary Source History of the Canal That Changed America*. New York, NY: The Rosen Publishing Group, Inc., 2001.

McCormick, Anita Louise. *The Industrial Revolution in American History*. Berkeley Heights, NJ: Enslow Publishers, 1998.

Wickes, Angela. *A Farm Through Time*. New York, NY: Dorling Kindersley Publishing, 2001.

Index

About the Author

Greg Roza has been writing history books for young students since 1999, including his most recent titles that explore in detail the cultures of several Native American groups such as the Iroquois, the Hopewell, and the Adena. Roza has a bachelor's and a master's degree in English from the State University of New York at Fredonia.

Photo Credits: Cover (left) © AP/Wide World Photos; cover (right), p. 40 (left and right) courtesy of The Library of Congress; pp. 5, 9 (left), 14–15, 31, 33, 35, 37, 39 © Bettmann/Corbis; p. 7 © Dave G. Houser/Corbis; p. 9 (right) © Lake County Museum; p. 10 © Hulton Archive/Getty Images; p. 13 © Kevin Fleming/Corbis; pp. 17, 18–19, 20–21 © Perry-Castañeda Library Map Collection/Historical Maps of the Americas/The University of Texas at Austin; p. 23 © Nelson Sá; p. 25 © Hulton–Deutsch Collection/Corbis; p. 27 © Medford Historical Society Collection; p. 29 Minnesota Historical Society/Corbis.

Designer: Nelson Sá; Editor: Joann Jovinelly; Photo Researcher: Nelson Sá